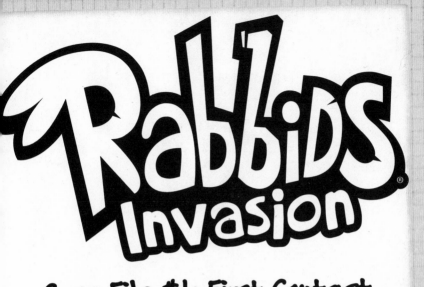

Case File #1: First Contact

by David Lewman

illustrated by Patrick Spaziante

Simon Spotlight

New York London Toronto Sydney New Delhi

Based on the TV series Rabbids™ Invasion as seen on Nickelodeon™

SIMON SPOTLIGHT
An imprint of Simon & Schuster Children's Publishing Division
1230 Avenue of the Americas, New York, New York 10020
First Simon Spotlight edition July 2014
© 2014 Ubisoft Entertainment. All rights reserved. Rabbids, Ubisoft, and the Ubisoft logo are trademarks of Ubisoft Entertainment in the U.S. and/or other countries.
All rights reserved, including the right of reproduction in whole or in part in any form.
SIMON SPOTLIGHT and colophon are registered trademarks of Simon & Schuster, Inc.
For information about special discounts for bulk purchases, please contact Simon & Schuster Special Sales at 1-866-506-1949 or business@simonandschuster.com.
Manufactured in the United States of America 0614 FFG
10 9 8 7 6 5 4 3 2 1
ISBN 978-1-4814-0038-1 (hc)
ISBN 978-1-4814-0037-4 (pbk)
ISBN 978-1-4814-0039-8 (eBook)

CHAPTER 1:

THEY'RE BACK!!!

Late one night a weird, eerie light lit up an empty field.

Since the field was empty, no one looked up to see where the weird light was coming from.

But if there HAD been people in the field, they certainly would have looked up. And seen . . .

A giant yellow submarine! Well, actually, it was a spaceship *shaped* like a giant yellow submarine.

The spaceship landed in the field with a loud THUMP! (That no one heard.) Then the door opened with a WHOOSH! (Also not heard.) Out stepped three Rabbids.

Rabbids? What are Rabbids?

They look a little like rabbits, but bigger. Instead of hopping on four legs, they walk on two. And while rabbits are quiet, gentle, and sweet, Rabbids . . . aren't.

The Rabbids had been visiting Earth for many, many years. And now they were back.

What did they want?

A very good question . . .

One of the Rabbids walked up to a small tree. He raised his hand and said, "Bwah bwah bwaaaaah!"

The tree said nothing. Because, you know, it was a tree.

The Rabbid stood there waiting for the tree to answer. After a moment, he grabbed the little tree and shook it. "BWAAAAH!"

BONK!

A pinecone, surprisingly big for such a small tree, fell on another Rabbid's head. The other Rabbids pointed and laughed. The Rabbid who had been bonked on the head glared at them, and they shut up.

The first Rabbid picked up the pinecone, looked at it, sniffed it, and popped it in his mouth. Not bad. *CRUNCH CRUNCH CRUNCH! GULP. BUUUUURRP!*

One of the other Rabbids noticed the glowing lights of a nearby city. Excited, he pointed and said, "Bwoooooh!"

The other Rabbids turned and saw what he was pointing at. They all started running toward the city.

CHAPTER 2:
AGENT GLYKER

In that very same city Agent Glyker arrived at work early one morning.

He stepped into his tiny office, looked around, and smiled. Not because it was a nice office. It wasn't. In fact, most people who stepped into Agent Glyker's office would probably say, "This office is ugly. With crummy furniture. And no windows. I would like to leave now."

But Agent Glyker loved his office because

it meant he was a real secret agent. In fact this morning when he opened the door to his office, he said it out loud: "I'm a real secret agent!"

He'd wanted to be a secret agent since he was a young boy. Just that week, Glyker had finally landed a job with the SGAII-RD (the Secret Government Agency for the Investigation of Intruders—Rabbid Division).

Agent Glyker leaned back in his beat-up old chair, daydreaming. Soon he'd crack a big case. Get promoted. Get a raise. Get a . . .

"GLYKER!"

BANG!!! Glyker fell backward in his chair, smacking the floor. Embarrassed, he looked up and saw his boss, Director Stern, standing in the door glaring at him.

"Yes, Director Stern?" Glyker asked, scrambling to his feet.

"You read all those files on the Rabbids?" Stern asked, pointing at the tall stack of files on Glyker's desk.

"Oh, yes, sir!" Glyker said, nodding. "I high-lighted the important parts, using a system of different colors. Blue for physical descriptions, green for theories about why the Rabbids are here, pink for—"

"Think you're ready to check out the next Rabbid call that comes in?" Stern interrupted, scowling. "Could be any day now."

"Definitely, sir!" Agent Glyker answered enthusiastically. He thought about saluting, but decided not to. Saluting might make Director Stern even grouchier. If that were possible.

Director Stern looked as though he seriously doubted Glyker was ready for anything. Shaking his head, he growled, "Okay, the next call's yours. Try not to blow it!"

Agent Glyker beamed. "Thank you, sir! You can count on me!"

Stern rolled his eyes. "I've got no choice. Everyone else is sick or on vacation." He didn't tell Glyker it was getting harder and harder to find agents who were willing to go anywhere *near* the Rabbids.

Stern stomped out. Agent Glyker grinned. His first Rabbid call! Any day now!

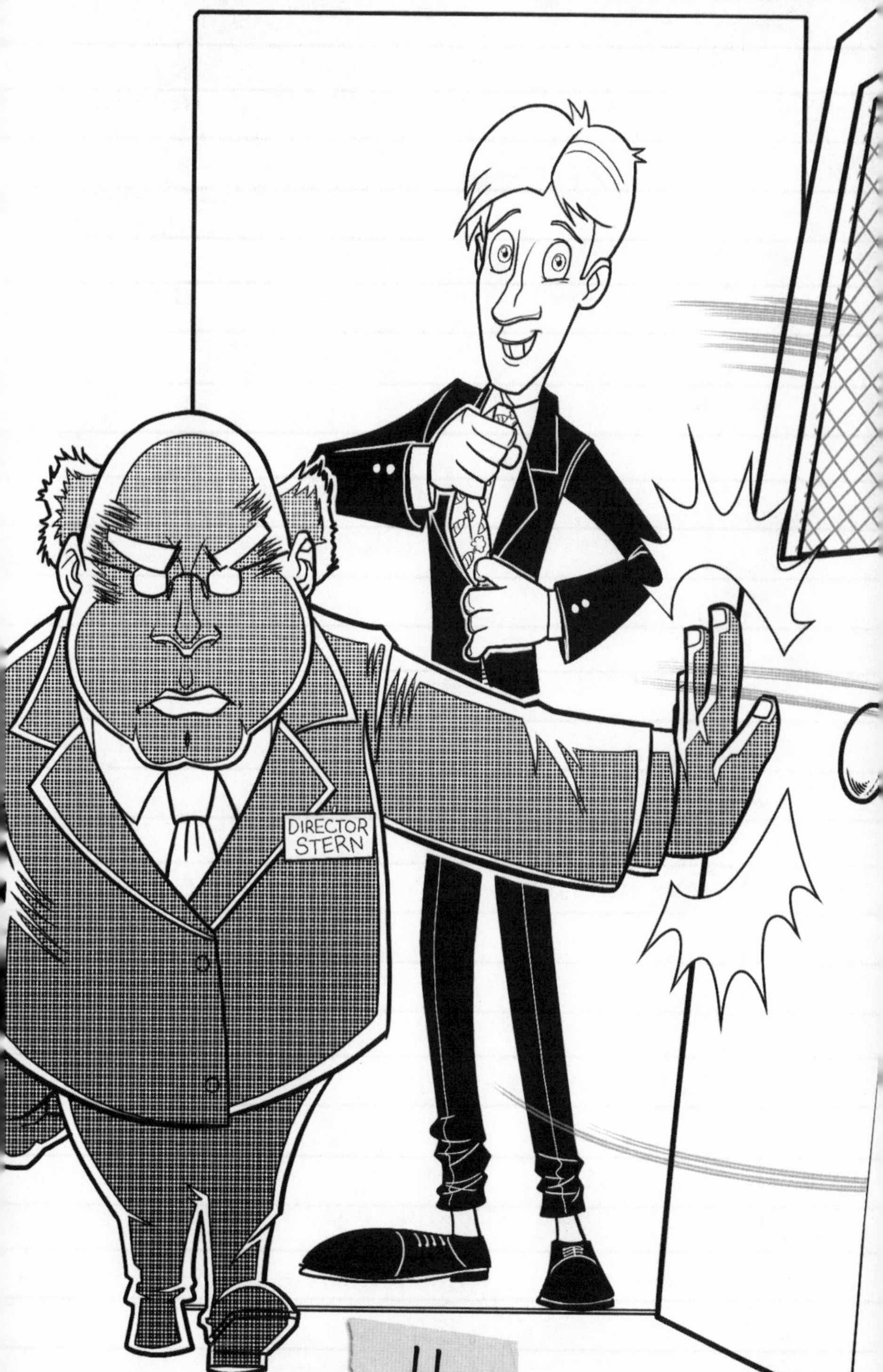
DIRECTOR
STERN

CHAPTER 3:

ANY DAY NOW

The Rabbids were happily running through an alley when one of them spotted something.

"Bwoooah!" he said, pointing up in the sky.

His fellow Rabbids looked up. On top of a building under construction, a crane was swinging a steel beam into place.

"Bwaaah . . . ," they murmured, impressed. The first Rabbid hurried toward the construction site and the other Rabbids followed.

A puzzled construction worker turned to his buddy. "Hey, Frank," he said. "Have you seen my jackhammer?"

"No, Mike, I haven't," Frank said. "But I *hear* it."

Sure enough, Mike and Frank could hear the BANG-BANG-BANG-BANG-BANG of a jackhammer hitting concrete. Mike ran toward the earsplitting sound and saw . . .

A Rabbid riding his jackhammer across a concrete floor!

"BWHEEEE!" shrieked the Rabbid, bouncing
and banging across the formerly smooth floor.

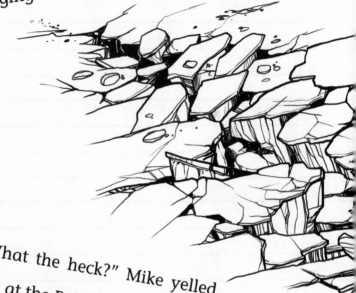

"What the heck?" Mike yelled,
staring at the Rabbid.

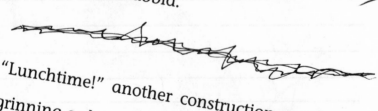

"Lunchtime!" another construction worker said,
grinning as he opened his big lunch box.

But the lunch box was empty.

"Hey!" he shouted. "Who stole my lunch?!"

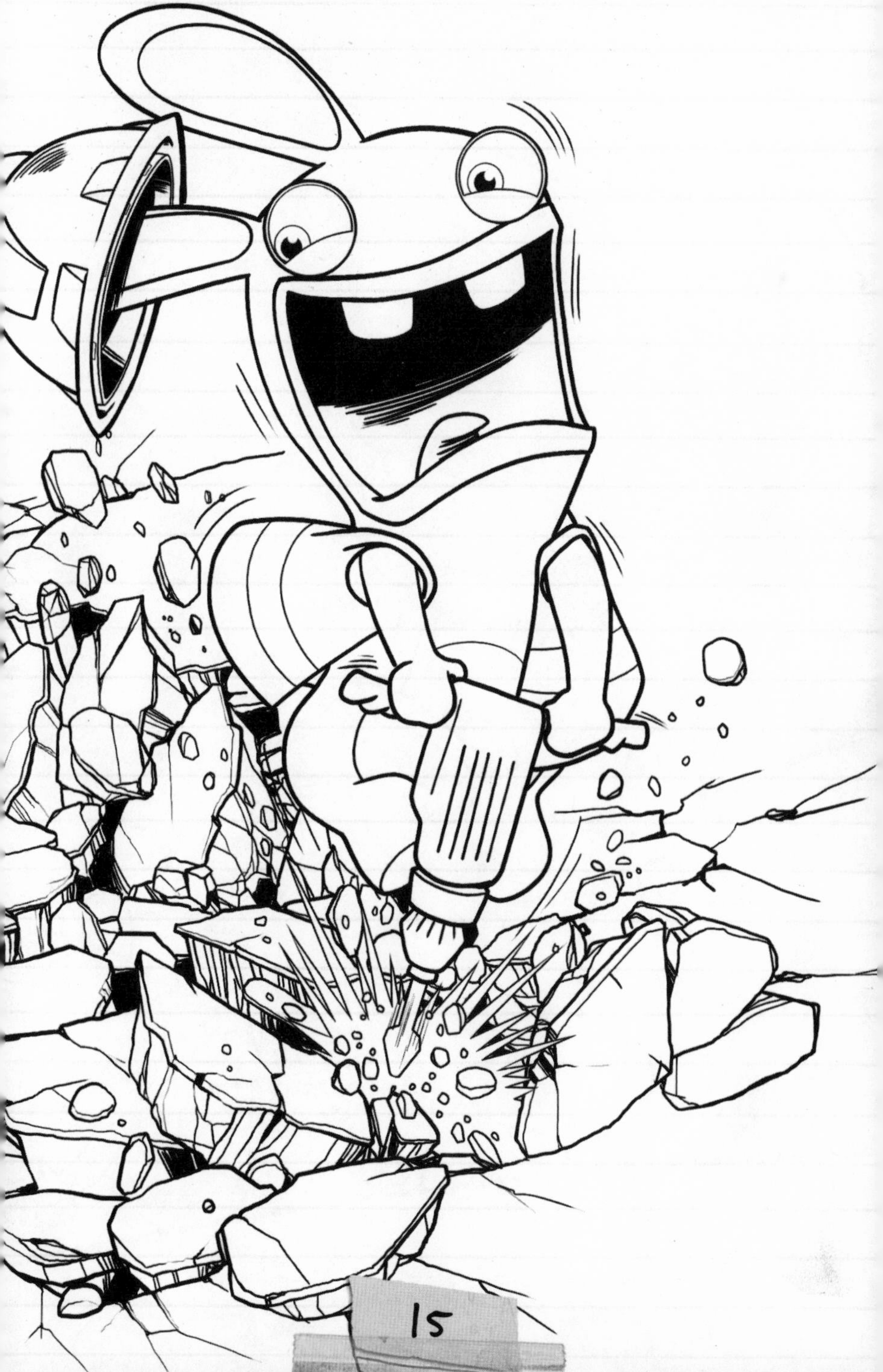

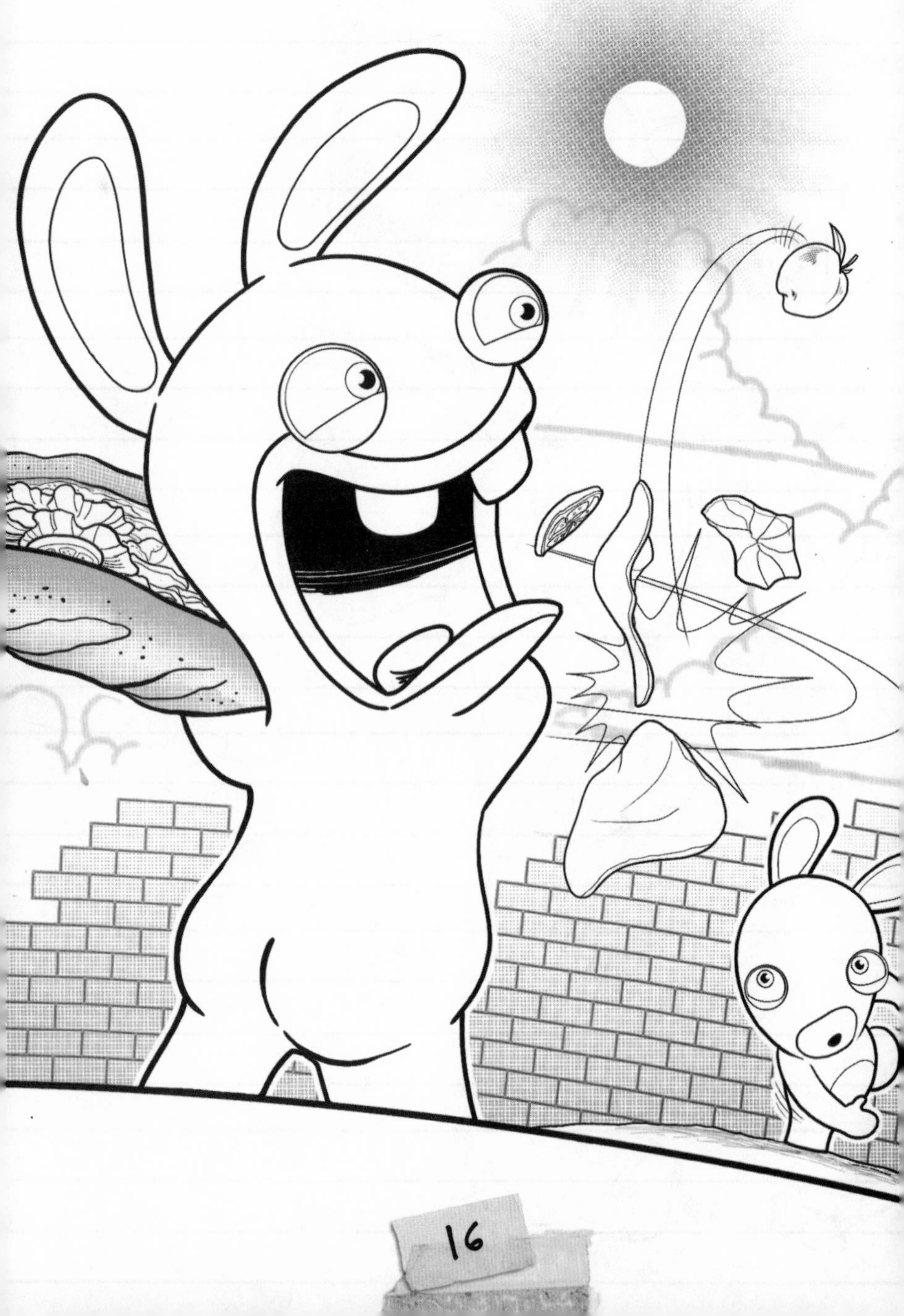

Behind a partly finished wall, a Rabbid reared back and hurled a green apple as hard as he could. Another Rabbid swung a long sub sandwich, batting the apple right back at the pitcher.

SHWOOP! The apple went straight into the pitching Rabbid's mouth.

"BWAAH HAAA HAAAA!" the batting Rabbid laughed.

The pitching Rabbid looked surprised but then swallowed the apple whole. *GULP! BUURRRPPP!*

A foreman caught up with another construction worker. "Rubin!" he yelled. "Put your hard hat back on!"

Rubin looked confused. "I've *got* it on, boss,"

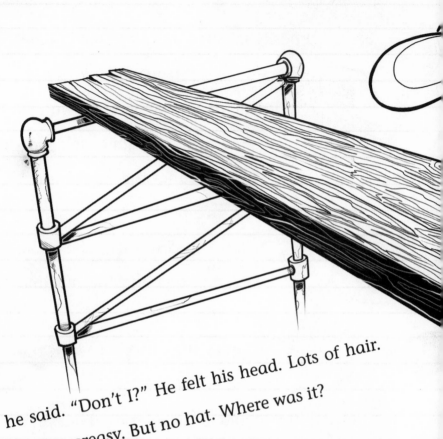

he said. "Don't I?" He felt his head. Lots of hair. Slightly greasy. But no hat. Where was it?

"BWHEEEEE!"

A Rabbid went zipping down a nearby ramp, riding on Rubin's hard hat.

"Hey!" Rubin shouted. "Come back here!"

As Rubin dashed after the Rabbid in his hat, the foreman whipped out his cell phone.

"Give me the Secret Government Agency for the Investigation of Intruders," he said. "Rabbid Division." Then he realized his phone didn't work that way, so he looked up the number and dialed it himself.

CHAPTER 4:
GLYKER'S FIRST RABBID CALL

Agent Glyker pulled up to the construction site in his crummy, beat-up brown car. He jumped out and ran up to the foreman, holding out his ID.

"Agent Glyker, SGAII-RD," he explained, loving the sound of it. "What's the problem?"

"What's the *problem*?!" the frustrated foreman bellowed. "Stolen hats! Stolen tools! Even stolen desserts! *MY DESSERT!*"

Glyker pulled out his notebook and started

jotting down notes for his case file. "Any luck capturing the suspects?" he asked.

The foreman shook his head. "No way. They're too quick. And slippery. And . . . unpredictable. Nothing they do makes any sense!"

"Where are they now?" Glyker asked.

The foreman shrugged. "Who knows? Probably somewhere figuring out a way to steal the whole building!"

"Not on my watch," Agent Glyker said determinedly as he headed into the construction site. Then he paused and turned back. "By the way, what will this building be when it's finished?"

The foreman snorted. "If it ever gets finished, it'll be the new library."

Library? Glyker thought to himself. *Why are the Rabbids trying to sabotage the library before it's even finished?*

Agent Glyker crept through the construction site looking for Rabbids. He ran from one spot to the next, hiding behind pillars and walls, peeking around for signs of Rabbids.

Nothing.

Glyker scratched his head. Where were they? Had they left? If he could catch a glimpse of one Rabbid, it'd make his day.

He caught a glimpse all right.

As he was standing on the ground floor pondering his next move, he heard a loud *VRRROOOM!* He whipped around and saw a piece of heavy equipment (it was called a front loader, but Glyker didn't know that) headed straight toward him!

Through the front loader's windshield, Glyker saw who was driving—Rabbids! Well, not driving exactly. No one was steering. But the Rabbids were making the front loader go faster and faster.

Glyker didn't have time to be excited about seeing an actual Rabbid. He turned and ran. The front loader followed him. He zigged. The front loader zigged. He zagged. The front loader (you guessed it) zagged too.

Then . . . *SPLORK!* Looking back over his shoulder at the front loader, Glyker ran right into a big patch of wet cement. He tried to pull his feet free, but the cement was too heavy.

The front loader was bearing down on him . . .

But at the last second it veered away, crashed into a wall, and came to a halt. The Rabbids jumped out of the front loader and ran off.

24

Well, I guess my day is made, Glyker thought as he watched them go. He kept trying to pull his feet out of the drying cement. In the distance, he could hear what sounded like crazed laughter . . .

"BWAAH HAA HAAAA!"

CHAPTER 5:
GLYKER'S REPORT

Agent Glyker trudged down the hallway at the SGAII-RD. *SHPLOP, SHPLOOP, SHPLOP, SHPLOOP . . .*

He left a trail of wet cement footprints behind him.

Director Stern stuck his head out his office (which was much nicer than Glyker's office). "GLYKER! Stop tracking that gunk all over the floor!"

Glyker turned around. "Yes, sir," he said, saluting in spite of himself. "Sir, I saw Rabbids!"

"Did you catch one?" Stern asked.

"No," Glyker admitted.

"Then get back out there and bring me a Rabbid!" he roared. "But first, clean up this mess!"

After Glyker had managed to scrape up most of the cement, he sat down in his office, pulled out his pocket notebook, and started typing on his lousy old computer.

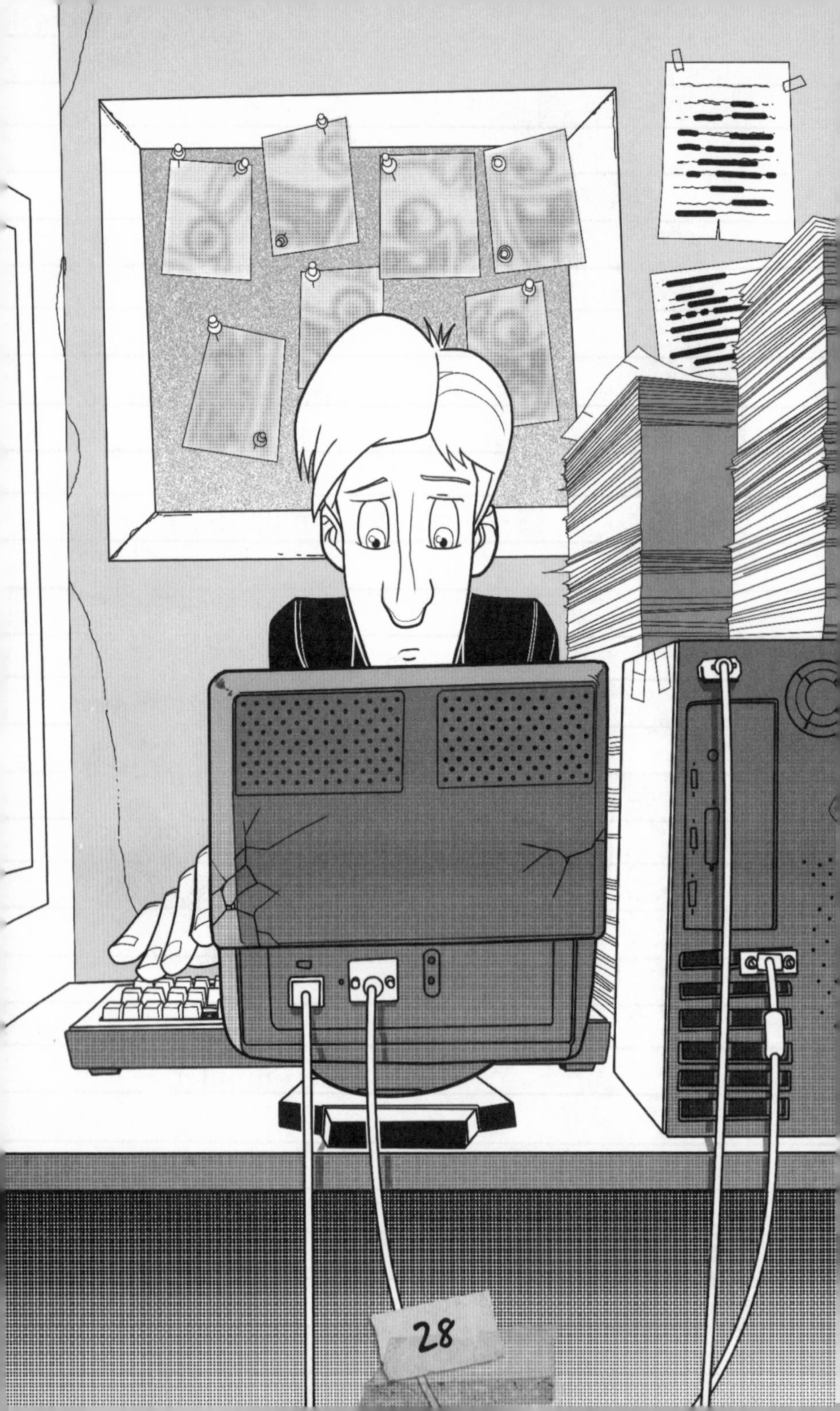
28

AGENT GLYKER'S REPORT

Today I, Agent Glyker, had my first encounter with Rabbids. Learned several things that might prove useful:

- Though they resemble rabbits, Rabbids are bigger. And much more dangerous.

- The Rabbids are interested in stealing hats, tools, and desserts.

- The Rabbids can drive construction vehicles. They're good at accelerating, but terrible at steering.

- Their laughter sounds like "bwah ha ha."

Summary: They chose to invade the unfinished library. Is this part of some larger plan to prevent people from reading and learning? Is there a book in the library that holds the key to who the Rabbids are and what their master plan is?

Glyker looked away from the dusty little screen of his computer. If he'd had a window, he would have gazed out, thinking. Instead, he stared at a stain on the wall.

What were the Rabbids up to? If they could invade the library, what might be next? His mom's house?

A scary thought occurred to Agent Glyker. Could the Rabbids be planning to take over the *world*?

Glyker clenched his jaw. *Not on my watch*, he thought. Then he smiled, thinking, *If I save the whole world, they'll have to give me a promotion. And a raise.* He looked around. *And a nicer office.*

But first he'd have to stop the Rabbids. Where were they now? And what were they doing?

31

CHAPTER 6:

WHAT THEY WERE DOING

The Rabbids peered through a chain-link fence at the town's swimming pool. They didn't know what it was, but they sure liked the way the water sparkled in the sunshine.

"Bwoooh," they all said. But how were they supposed to get over the tall fence?

One of the Rabbids (who seemed to be the leader) got another Rabbid to lean against the fence, facing in toward the pool. Then he got the third Rabbid to climb up on the first Rabbid's shoulders.

"Bwuh!" complained the bottom Rabbid as the leader clambered up the two Rabbids and flipped over the fence.

From the inside, the leader gestured for the other two Rabbids to hurry up and follow him.

The top Rabbid managed to jump up and grab the top of the fence. Grunting, he hoisted himself up and over.

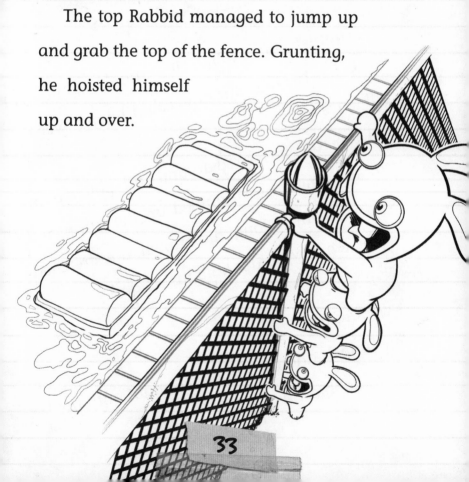

That left one Rabbid. He certainly didn't want to be left behind. But how could he get over the tall fence all by himself?

Desperate, he looked around and spotted a tree near the fence. He shimmied up the trunk and scooted out onto a long thin branch that stretched over the fence. Would it hold his weight?

Nope.

CRRRRACK!

The branch and the Rabbid fell right onto the other two Rabbids! WHUMP!

34

The three Rabbids stood up and shook themselves.
They were in!

"Mom?" asked a little boy near the kiddie pool.
"Where are my swimming goggles?"

"I don't know," his mom said without looking up from her magazine. "Maybe you forgot to bring them."

"No, I just had them!" the boy wailed. "They were right here! WHERE ARE MY GOGGLES?"

Nearby, a Rabbid sneaked away wearing goggles. But not on his head. They were around his chest, looking a little like a bikini top.

"Dad, where's the sunblock?" asked a little girl near the shallow end of the pool.

36

"I don't know, honey," her dad answered. "It was right here."

A few steps away, a Rabbid ran up to another Rabbid and squirted him in the face with sunblock. *SHPLORRRP!!!*

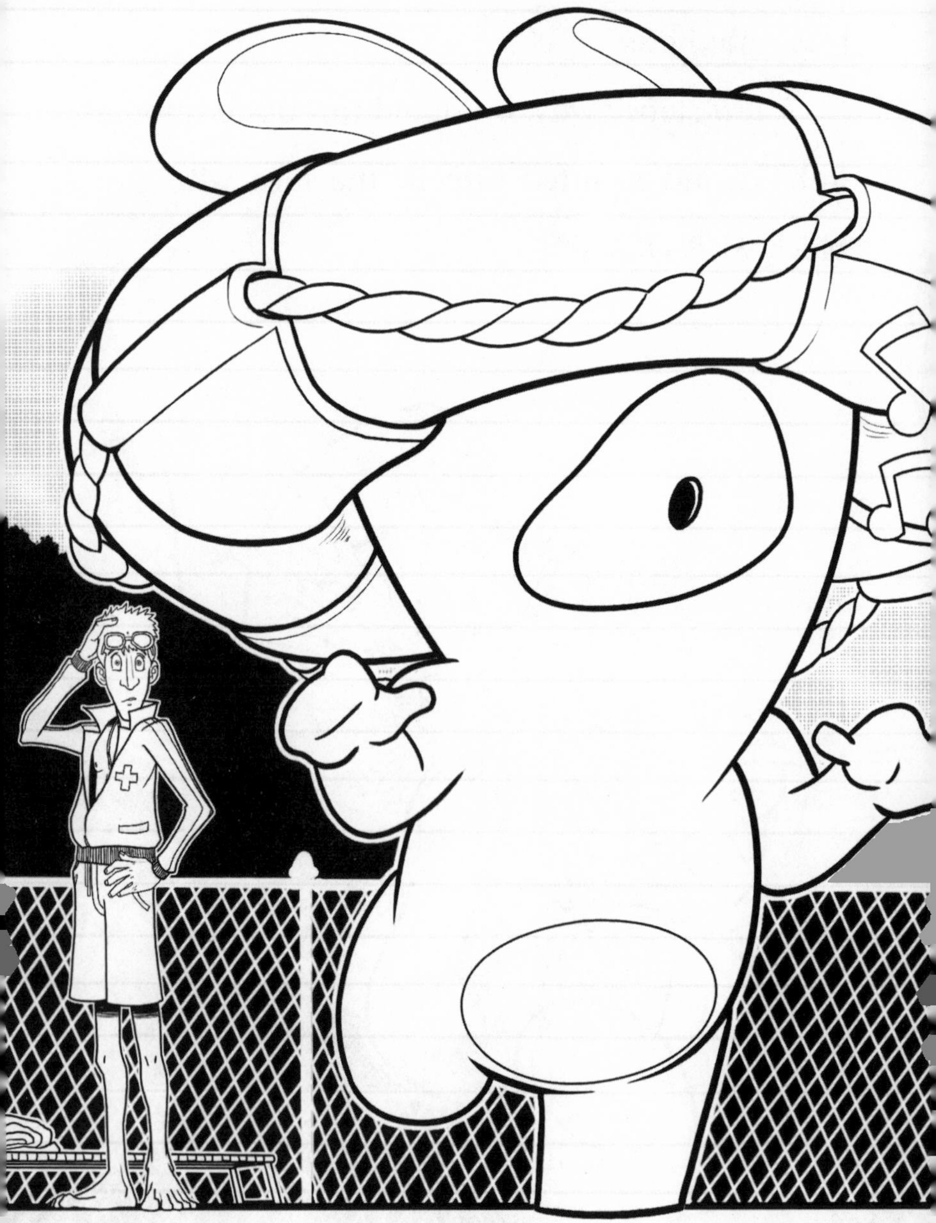

"BWAAH HA HA HAAA!" the first Rabbid laughed as he ran off. The sunblocked Rabbid tried to chase him but couldn't see where he was going and landed right in the pool. *SPLOOOSH!*

"That's weird," said one lifeguard to another. "The life preserver that's usually right here isn't here."

He didn't notice the Rabbid behind him, sneaking away wearing the life preserver on his head.

The two lifeguards ran in to the pool manager's office. "Mr. Decker!" they cried.

Startled, the manager looked up from his science fiction fan magazine. "Shouldn't you two be in your chairs blowing your whistles?" he barked.

"We're getting, like, a *million* complaints," the first lifeguard blurted out.

"All kinds of stuff has gone missing," the second lifeguard explained. "Including one of our life preservers. And there have been . . . sightings."

"Sightings of what?" Mr. Decker asked, excited. "Aliens? Vampires? Zombies?"

The two lifeguards looked at each other. Neither one wanted to say it.

"WELL?" Mr. Decker bellowed.

The first lifeguard swallowed. "Big rabbits," he finally admitted. "One of them was wearing some kind of bikini."

Mr. Decker raised his eyebrows and reached for the phone.

CHAPTER 7:

NO RUNNING!

Agent Glyker drove to the swimming pool as fast as he could without speeding. (If secret agents speed, they get tickets just like everyone else.)

A crowd of annoyed people stood around the entrance. Some were wrapped in towels. Others just dripped on the sidewalk.

"I *hate* adult swim!" a little boy cried.

Glyker spotted a lifeguard and hurried up to

him, displaying his ID. "Where are the Rabbids?" he asked.

"They're somewhere in there." He pointed toward the pool. "We've cleared everybody out."

Agent Glyker started to run toward the pool.

TWEEET! "NO RUNNING!"

Glyker stopped and looked around. The lifeguard shrugged, holding his whistle. "Sorry," he said. "Habit."

Glyker continued through the locker room. When he reached the door leading to the pool area, he cracked it open and peeked outside.

There they were. But they looked . . . different.

One Rabbid gleefully tore pages from a fashion magazine and then stuck the rest of the magazine to the globs of sunblock on his head. Another wore a life preserver as a hat. The third was wearing swimming goggles like a bikini top.

They seemed thrilled to have the pool all to themselves, though they also seemed to have no idea what to do with it.

Sunblock and Life Preserver Hat (as Glyker thought of them at that moment) started picking up deck chairs and tossing them into the pool. They sounded as though they were counting while they swung the chairs back and forth before letting them go: "Bwah . . . bway . . . bwee!" *SPLOOSH!* "BWAH HA HA HA HA!"

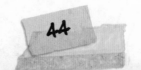

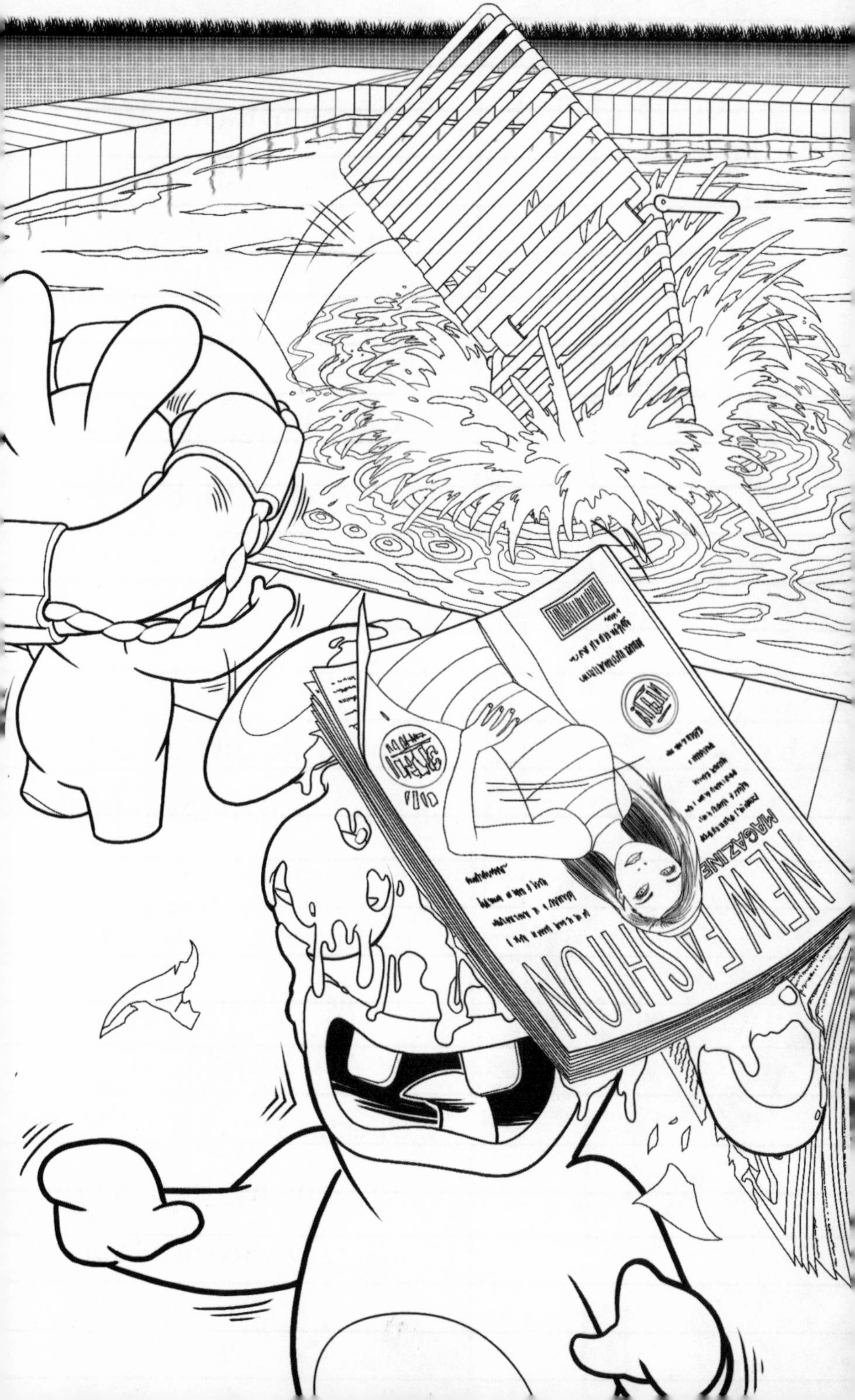

NEW FASHION
MAGAZINE

Watching them, Agent Glyker had lost track of the third Rabbid. Where was Bikini Goggles? Glyker looked around . . .

And there he was! Standing on the high dive, staring down into the clear blue water.

All by himself. He now had a big blob of sunscreen on his head that looked like whipped cream on top of a sundae.

Could Glyker capture him? And bring him back to Director Stern?

He could try. He had to.

Glyker waited until Sunblock and Life Preserver Hat walked away to grab another chair. Staying low, he scurried across the hot concrete to the high dive ladder.

As he quietly climbed the rungs of the ladder, he could hear the other two Rabbids flinging furniture. "Bwah . . . bway . . . bwee!" *SPLOOSH!* "BWAH HA HA HA HA!"

Finally Glyker reached the top of the ladder. He peeked over the end of the diving board.

The Rabbid was still there. But he was starting to lean over the edge of the board. At any second, he might drop into the water.

It was now or never!

Glyker hauled himself up onto the diving board and ran toward Bikini Goggles. He was about to grab the Rabbid from behind . . .

. . . when the creature whipped around, gasped in surprise ("Bwaa?"), and jumped over Glyker . . .

. . . who couldn't stop himself and ran right off the end of the board. (He might have been able to stop himself if the diving board wasn't now covered in slippery, slimy sunscreen that had fallen off the Rabbid's head. But then again . . . probably not.)

"AAAAHHHHH!" he screamed as he plum-
meted through the air.

BLOOOSHH! Glyker hit the water headfirst and
sank all the way to the bottom. He pushed off the
pool floor, shot to the surface, and gasped for air.

Treading water as best he could in his soaked
clothes, he looked around.

No Rabbids. They were gone.

As he climbed out of the pool, dripping wet, Agent Glyker thought, *First they invade our library. Then our public pool. What's next?*

CHAPTER 8:

WHAT'S NEXT

At the end of a long hard day working at the zoo, the zookeeper locked the front gate and headed home.

But three special visitors were still inside.

The Rabbids slowly emerged from the bushes. They wandered through the zoo, amazed by every animal they saw.

They tried to open their mouths as wide as the hippopotamus. This just made their jaws ache.

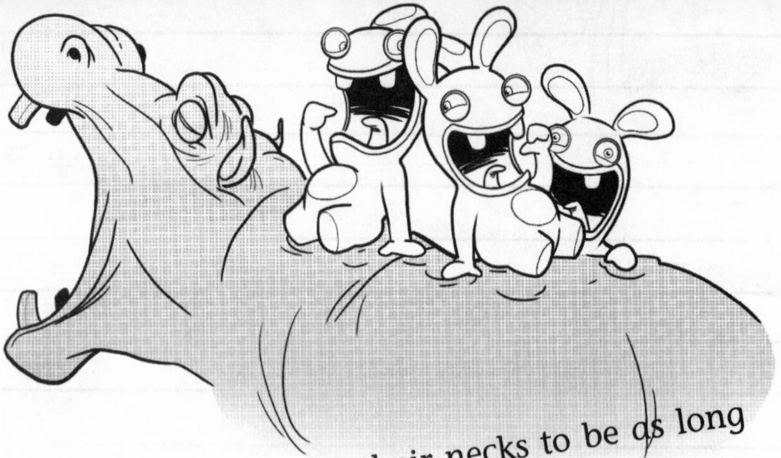

They tried to stretch their necks to be as long as the giraffe's. But then they realized they didn't really have necks.

They tried talking to the monkeys. "Bwah!" said the Rabbid leader, holding up his hand in greeting. "Bwah bwah bwah!"

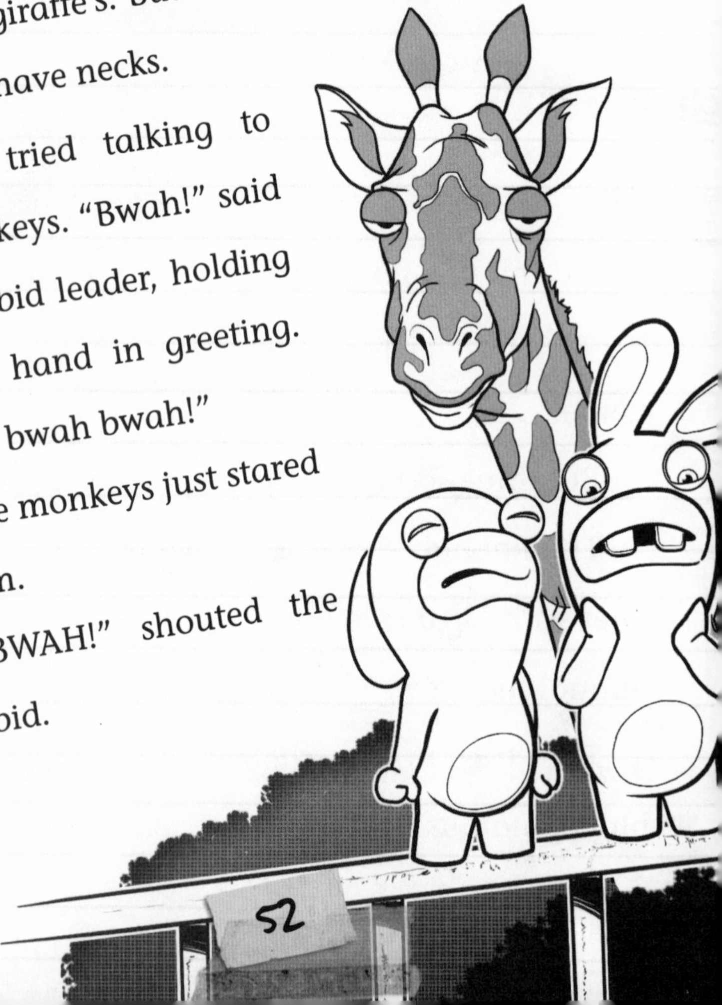

The monkeys just stared at him.

"BWAH!" shouted the Rabbid.

"Ooh ooh! Aah aah! Ee ee! Oo WAAAHHH!" screamed the monkeys.

They talked back to the monkeys. "Bwhooh bwhooh! Bwaah Bwaah! Bwee Bwee! Bwoo BWAAAHH!"

The monkeys started swinging around on the ropes in their cage. That looked fun! The Rabbids jumped up and started swinging through the zoo's trees, leaping from branch to branch.

But their short arms soon grew tired. The leader dropped to the ground, and the other two Rabbids

landed behind him, breathing heavily.

"Bwoooooh!" the leader exclaimed, looking at the big animal caged in front of them.

It was a magnificent lion with a full, dark mane and a long tail.

When the lion noticed the three Rabbids staring at him, he roared. "ROOAAARRR!"

The Rabbids jumped back, startled. Then they opened their mouths and roared back. "BWOOOAAARRR!"

The lion started pacing back and forth, walking from one end of his cage to the other, staring at the bizarre creatures on the other side of the black bars.

The Rabbids watched the lion pacing. The cage didn't seem big enough for such a huge beast. They looked at each other and nodded in agreement.

This animal needed more room . . .

CHAPTER 9:

ZOOM TO THE ZOO!

That evening Agent Glyker stayed late in his crummy little office working on his report. A puddle of pool water dripped off his sopping-wet clothing onto the floor around his broken old chair.

AGENT GLYKER'S REPORT (CONTINUED)

- Rabbids are **NOT** afraid of heights.

- They're good jumpers, just like the rabbits they resemble.

- They like to throw chairs in pools.

- They're hard to catch.

- They seem to like to wear things on their heads, including life preservers, magazines, and sunblock.

Summary: After invading a place of learning, the Rabbids chose to invade a place of leisure. What does this mean?

Agent Glyker stopped typing and read over his notes. His observation that the Rabbids liked to wear things on their heads caught his attention. That was a particularly clever observation, if he did say so himself. Could this information somehow help him capture a Rabbid?

He was afraid that if he didn't catch a Rabbid soon, he'd be fired.

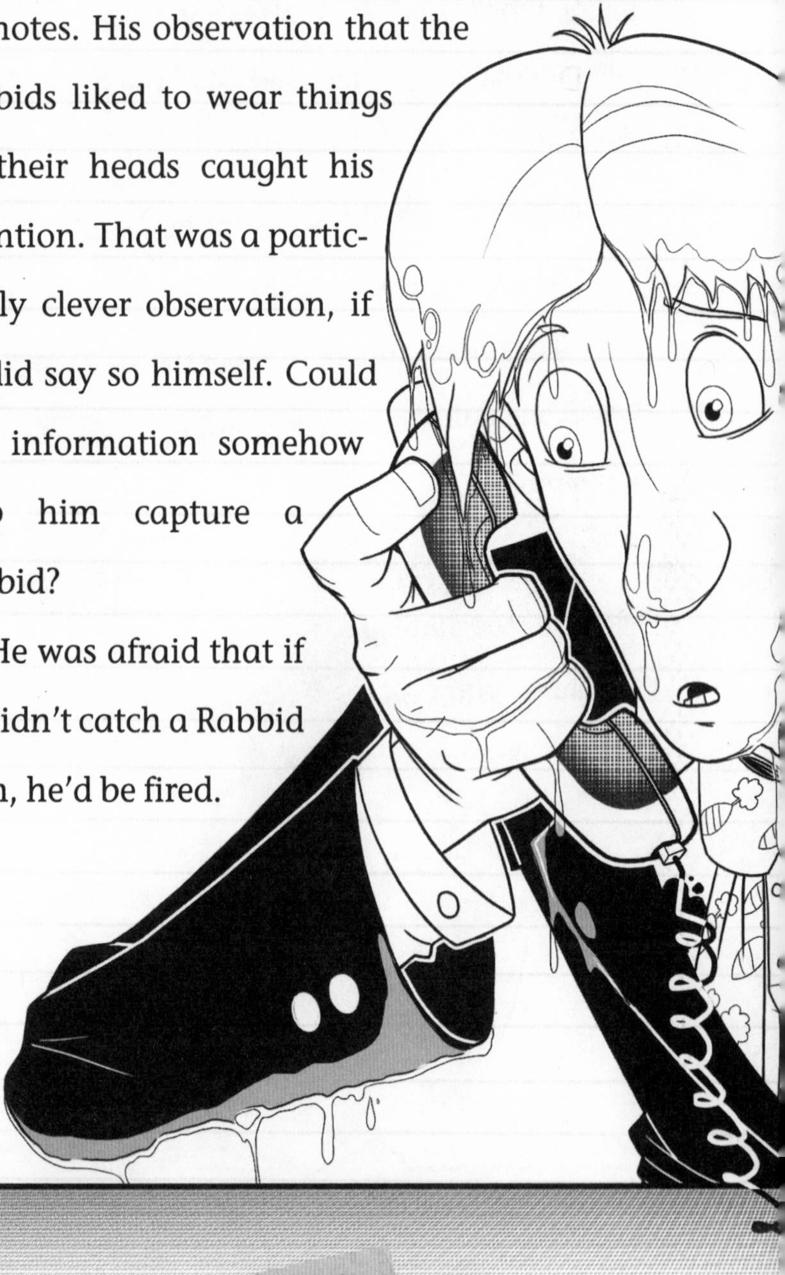

Director Stern had hinted as much that afternoon.

Here's what his hint sounded like: "GLYKER, IF YOU DON'T CATCH A RABBID SOON, YOU'RE *FIRED!*"

The ugly old brown phone on his desk rang. *BRRRRING!* As soon as he picked it up, he heard his boss's voice blaring, "GLYKER! Have you got the TV on?"

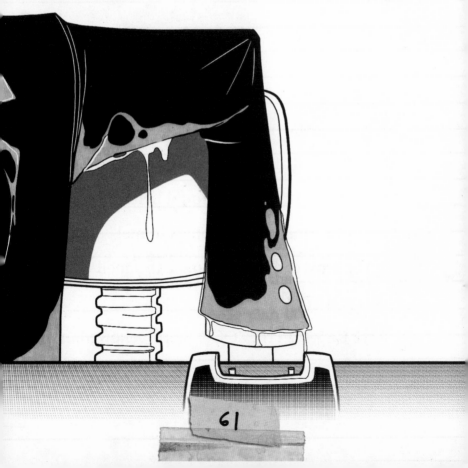

"There's no TV in my office, Director Stern."

Stern ignored this. "There's some kind of disturbance down at the zoo. You'd better get down there pronto. Smells like Rabbids to me!"

Glyker was confused. "You can smell things through your TV?"

"JUST GET TO THE ZOO!" Stern bellowed, and hung up.

Agent Glyker stood up, slipped in the puddle of pool water, and fell. *WHAM!* He got up and hurried down the hall toward the exit, rubbing his sore butt.

But as he passed the Closet of Super-Secret Spy Gadgets, he paused. Since he was new, he wasn't authorized to take anything out of the closet without special permission.

But what was the point of being a spy if you couldn't use super-secret gadgets?

At the zoo's front gate Agent Glyker zipped over to the zookeeper and a policeman. "What's up?" he asked.

"Neighbors complained about roaring, howling, and screeching," the policeman said, consulting his notebook.

"Is that unusual at a zoo?" Glyker asked.

"We think some animals may be out of their cages," the cop continued.

"Did you go inside to check?" Glyker asked.

"Are you kidding?" the zookeeper exclaimed. "That'd be incredibly dangerous!"

The zookeeper was right.

Glyker had only gone a few steps into the zoo when he spotted one of the Rabbids strolling along. He started after him but quickly noticed there was

something between him and the Rabbid. Something big, furry, and white.

A polar bear!

Glyker froze. Though furry and cute looking, polar bears were *extremely* dangerous. Luckily, the polar bear hadn't noticed him. When it turned its head away, Glyker dove behind a drinking fountain.

He cautiously looked out. The polar bear wandered off to another part of the zoo.

Glyker carefully made his way through the dark zoo, hoping to catch sight of another Rabbid.

He heard a *CRREEAK!* It sounded like a rusty gate opening. He investigated, and saw . . .

A rhinoceros stepping out of its enclosure!

Uh-oh.

Glyker froze again. Maybe if he didn't move, the rhino wouldn't notice—

"BWAAH!"

Glyker whipped around and saw a startled Rabbid. Before he could grab it, the Rabbid sprinted away, right past the rhino.

Now the rhino definitely noticed Glyker.

Pawing the ground, it lowered its head, aimed its long sharp horn right at him, and charged!

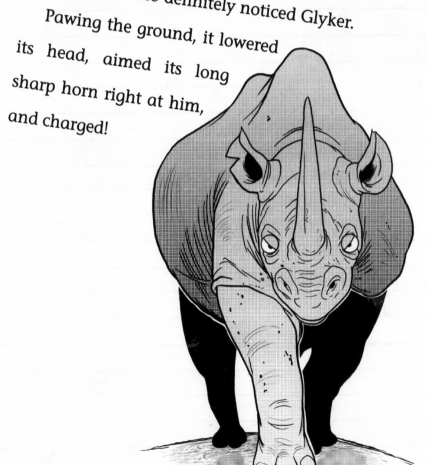

"WHOA!" Glyker yelled, putting his hands out, strongly suggesting that the rhino stop.

The rhino ignored this suggestion.

Glyker turned and scrambled up into the nearest tree. Lucky for him, rhinos can't see that well. The rhino ran past the tree, enjoying its freedom.

Glyker lowered himself to the ground and headed in the opposite direction from the rhino.

It seemed as though the Rabbids had let all these animals out of their cages. *Was this part of their master plan?* Glyker wondered.

He'd have to be extra careful.

First a polar bear, then a rhino . . .

And now a lion.

The huge lion was trying to open a concession stand with its claws. He must have smelled the food stored inside.

But just past the lion, on the other side of the

stand, were three Rabbids!

They looked like they were heading out of the zoo. There was no way Glyker could get past the lion and catch one of them.

But he wasn't going to lose them again. Not this time.

Thinking quickly, he pulled something out of his pocket and threw it at the Rabbids. Then he jumped into a trash can to hide.

The lion went on scratching at the concession stand.

The thing Glyker threw hit one of the Rabbids in the back of the head.

"Bwah?"

The Rabbid stopped and looked at the ground to see what had hit him.

It was a hat.

"Bwaaaah!" the Rabbid said, excited. He bent down, picked up the hat, and popped it on his head.

Then he hurried to catch up with his two fellow Rabbids and left the zoo.

Inside the trash can, Agent Glyker smiled. (Even though it really stank in there.)

CHAPTER 10

WHY HE SMILED

Once he'd gotten safely out of the zoo (barely avoiding a tiger, an elephant, and an ostrich), Agent Glyker pulled a small rectangular device out of his pocket.

BOOP! BOOP! BOOP!

The booping dot on the device's screen moved across a map of the city. It showed exactly where the Rabbids were. Glyker had attached a tiny transmitter to the hat he'd thrown at the Rabbids.

So now the transmitter was sending a signal to the device Glyker held in his hand.

This is more like it, Glyker thought. *Instead of chasing the Rabbids through construction sites and pools and zoos, I'll just wait for them to fall asleep. Then I'll sneak up on them.*

Staring at the device, Glyker climbed into his lousy old car.

The super-secret gadget led Glyker to the municipal dump on the edge of the city. The booping dot had stopped there. Glyker hoped that the Rabbids hadn't just thrown the hat in the dump and moved on. He was counting on their love of putting things on their heads.

And he was right.

Glyker turned off the booping sound and made

his way toward the signaling transmitter, carefully picking his way around the mounds of trash. Holding his nose, Glyker passed a big pile of used diapers. Suddenly, he spotted the hat.

And it was moving.

The Rabbid was still wearing it! And his two fellow Rabbids were nearby!

The three Rabbids looked very happy. As they picked through all the garbage, they made happy little sounds, almost as though they were humming to themselves. "Bwum bwa bwum bwa bweedly bwum . . ."

One picked up an old toaster. He stared into the two slots, turned it upside down, shook it, and tried wearing it on his head. He even licked it. Another found a shoe. He tried talking into it like a telephone. "Bwa bwah?" Tried hammering with it. Grabbed the shoelace and whirled it around his head. Let go and . . .

WHACK!

The shoe hit the Rabbid wearing Glyker's hat in the head. "BWAH HA HA HA!" laughed the Rabbid who'd thrown it.

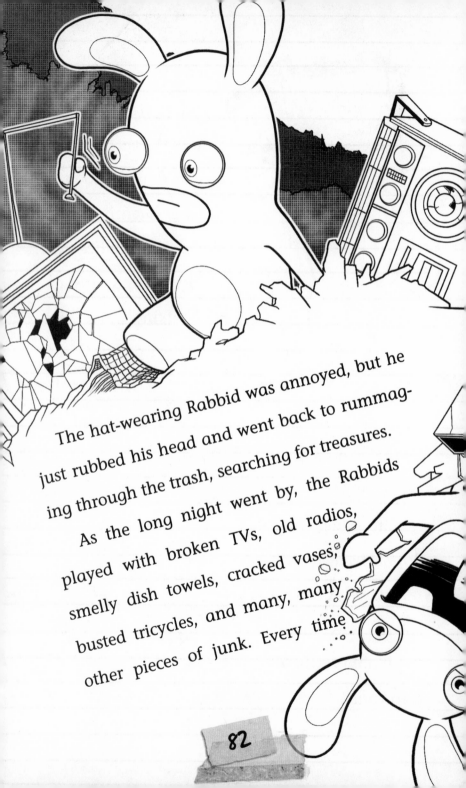

The hat-wearing Rabbid was annoyed, but he just rubbed his head and went back to rummaging through the trash, searching for treasures.

As the long night went by, the Rabbids played with broken TVs, old radios, smelly dish towels, cracked vases, busted tricycles, and many, many other pieces of junk. Every time

Glyker thought they were settling down to go to sleep, they found another broken object to mess around with.

And Glyker was getting sleepy . . .

Glyker woke with a start. The sun was coming up! He'd fallen asleep using a guitar case as a pillow and a wedding dress as a blanket.

Were the Rabbids gone? He looked around frantically and . . .

There they were! Fast asleep! Now was his chance!

He tiptoed over to the nearest Rabbid, who had

curled up on an old green sofa. He leaned over and grabbed the Rabbid!

"BWWAAAAAAAAHHHHH!!!"

As he tried to run back to his car carrying the Rabbid, its eyes turned red and it screamed. The Rabbid flailed its arms and kicked its legs, trying to climb onto Glyker's head.

"Calm down!" he said. "I'm not going to hurt you!"

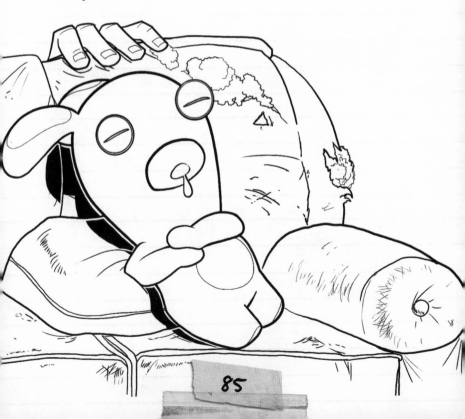

Then . . . *THWACK!* Something squishy hit Glyker in the back of the head. *THWACK! THWACK! THWACK!* Three more somethings hit him as he ran. Smelly somethings.

The other two Rabbids had awakened as soon as their fellow Rabbid screamed. They grabbed used diapers from the big pile and threw them at Glyker.

One of the used diapers landed in front of Glyker. He stepped right on it and . . . FWOOP! He slipped and fell.

Before he could get up and run to his car, the other two Rabbids reached Glyker and their captured cohort. They grabbed the Rabbid's arms and yanked him away from Glyker. As they ran away, Glyker saw one of the Rabbids pull an odd-looking device out and press a button on it.

"NO!" Glyker yelled after them desperately. "YOU'RE COMING WITH ME!"

But no one heard Agent Glyker yell, because his voice was completely drowned out by something much, much louder . . .

A spaceship.

CHAPTER 11:

THERE'S ALWAYS NEXT TIME

As Glyker watched helplessly, the spaceship landed right on top of the pile of used diapers. *SHPLUMP!*

The door opened and the three Rabbids ran inside. When the last one was in, he turned around, stuck his tongue out at Glyker, and made a very rude noise: *PPVRRRRPPP!*

The door closed and the spaceship flew away.

Back at the office Glyker finished telling Director Stern what had happened. For a moment his boss just sat in his big leather chair (which was much, much nicer than Glyker's chair), scowling.

"So you're telling me," he said slowly, "that the Rabbids got in a spaceship and flew away."

"Yes, sir," Agent Glyker said, nodding.

"And that's why you weren't able to catch one and bring it in for questioning," Stern continued.

"Right," Glyker said.

"But you didn't take any pictures of the spaceship," his boss said, sounding angrier with each sentence.

"Um, no," Glyker admitted. "I forgot."

"You forgot," Stern echoed in disbelief. "So tell me, Agent Glyker . . ."

"Yes, Director Stern?"

"WHY THE HECK SHOULDN'T I FIRE YOU RIGHT THIS INSTANT?" Stern roared.

Agent Glyker thought a moment. "Because," he said, "those Rabbids will be back. And when they return, I'm going to *get* them. For absolute sure this time!"

Stern looked unconvinced.

"Also," Glyker added, "I'm your nephew, Uncle Jim. Mom'd be really mad at you."

Stern wiped his face and shook his head. "Just get out of my office," he muttered.

Late that night on the other side of the city, a weird, eerie light lit up an empty field . . .

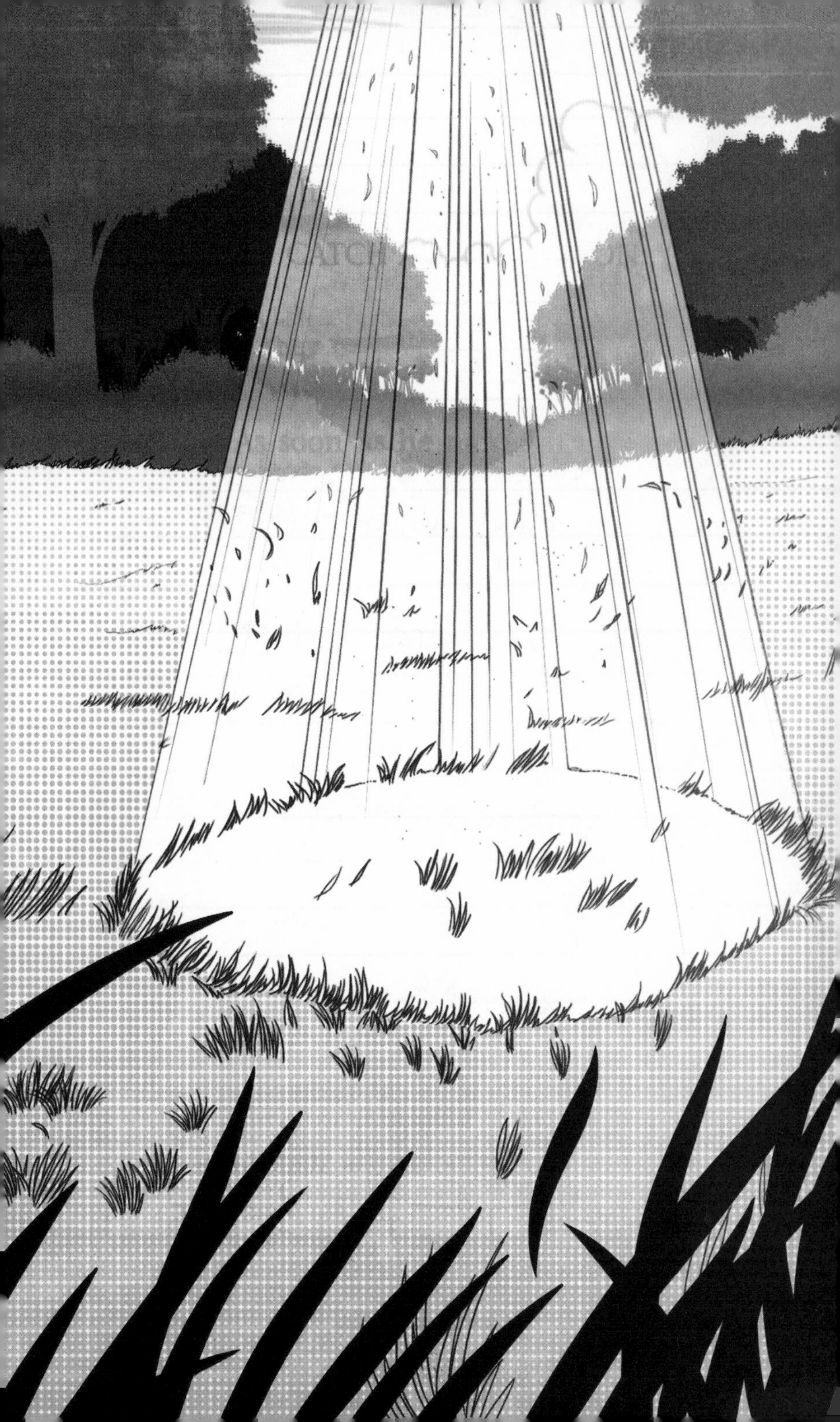

Attention !!!

Glyker's To-Do List:

1. Tell Mom to remind Uncle Jim that I'm his nephew.

2. Buy duct tape to fix office chair (and office ceiling, desk, and door.)

3. Ask Uncle Jim for nicer office.

4. Remember to call Uncle Jim "Director Stern" at the office.

5. Buy toilet paper.

large mouth

bent tongue